RACE CAR
RIVAL

SEP 2009

BY JAKE MADDOX

illustrated by Sean Tiffany

text by Chris Kreie

Impact Books are published by Stone Arch Books
151 Good Counsel Drive, P.O. Box 669
Mankato, Minnesota 56002
www.stonearchbooks.com

Library of Congress Cataloging-in-Publication Data
Maddox, Jake.
    Race car rival / by Jake Maddox; text by Chris Kreie;
    illustrated by Sean Tiffany.
    p. cm. — (Impact books. A Jake Maddox sports story
    (on the speedway))
    ISBN 978-1-4342-1601-4
    [1. Stock car racing—Fiction. 2. Automobile racing—Fiction.]
I. Kreie, Chris. II. Tiffany, Sean, ill. III. Title.
PZ7.M25643Rac 2010
[Fic]—dc22   2009004228

Creative Director: Heather Kindseth
Graphic Designer: Hilary Wacholz

Printed in the United States of America.

TABLE OF CONTENTS

CHAPTER 1

GO-KART GLORY

Shawn Lewis kept his kart just inches behind the go-kart in front of him. He shot down the track straightaway and into the last lap of the race.

"It's time, Freddy," Shawn said to himself. Freddy Stow was racing in the kart ahead of Shawn. "It's time for me to beat you again."

The crowd was going wild. There must have been 500 fans in the stands.

Shawn and the other drivers were competing in the Premiere Tire Cup. It was one of the most important kart races of the season.

The first person to cross the finish line would win $300. They'd also receive four brand new kart tires from Premiere Tire.

Shawn drove hard through the first turn. Then he stayed right behind Freddy's kart through corner number two.

The two karts sped down the back straightaway. Just two more corners before they crossed the finish line. The rest of the cars were too far back to catch them.

This is where you always make the same mistake, Freddy, thought Shawn. *You drive too sharp through the third corner and let me pass you.*

The two karts approached the third turn, Shawn took his foot off the accelerator for a split second. He drove his kart to the outside and went wide through the third turn. He positioned himself to drop tight through turn number four.

Everything went just like Shawn had planned. Freddy went sharp into turn three, which forced his kart out wide after the last turn. Shawn saw his chance and jumped at it. He pushed the pedal all the way to the floor and shot past Freddy on the last turn and into the final straightaway.

Seconds later Shawn crossed the finish line first. "Yes!" shouted Shawn. "I win again!"

After the race, the top three drivers waited in victory lane to receive their trophies.

"Good race, Freddy," said Shawn as he put his hand out.

Freddy shook Shawn's hand. "You too," said Freddy.

"What's it like always coming in second?" Shawn asked, laughing. "We're just like Johnny Pride and 'Mean' Gene Pederson."

Johnny Pride was Shawn's favorite professional stock car racer. He was everyone's favorite. He was young, good looking, and had won the Chase for the Cup three years in a row.

"I'm Johnny. I always finish first," teased Shawn. "And you're Mean Gene. You never seem to win."

Gene Pederson always finished behind Johnny Pride. He didn't have many fans.

In fact, he was the most hated driver in stock car racing. In a race last season, his car had rammed Johnny's into the wall. Johnny had ended up in the hospital, and his fans had never forgiven Mean Gene.

"I'm just joking, Freddy," said Shawn. "You need to smile once in a while. You always look mad, just like Mean Gene."

The boys received their trophies and walked off the track. "Guess where I'm going tomorrow?" said Shawn.

"Where?" asked Freddy.

"To Talladega! To a real NASCAR race!" said Shawn. "My uncle's company is a corporate sponsor. I get to be Johnny Pride's junior team member all week."

Shawn ran toward the track exit with the first place trophy in hand.

CHAPTER 2

AT THE TRACK

"Uncle Roy!" shouted Shawn as he stepped off the bus in front of Talladega Superspeedway.

"Hi, Shawn," said Roy. "Let me get a look at you. You've got to be six inches taller than the last time I saw you."

"Yeah, right, Uncle Roy," said Shawn. "You just saw me a few months ago."

"Doesn't matter," said Roy. "All I know is that you're growing like a weed."

He lifted up Shawn's baseball cap and messed his hair. Shawn grinned and rolled his eyes.

The two unloaded Shawn's bags from the bottom of the bus and walked across the street. "Check out my ride," said Roy.

"Is this yours?" asked Shawn. "Sweet."

The two of them climbed aboard Roy's golf cart. It was built to look like a mini stock car, and it was covered from front to back in Top Shelf Oil Filter logos.

"How do you like working for Top Shelf?" Shawn asked as the two of them cruised toward the speedway.

"It's the best job I've ever had," said Roy. "Plus, they let my favorite nephew be a junior race team member. Can't beat that, right?"

"That's right!" said Shawn.

The two of them drove through a tunnel under the Talladega track. They headed into the middle of the speedway.

"This is awesome, Uncle Roy," said Shawn. "I can't believe I'm here."

"You deserve it, Shawn," said Roy. "Your dad tells me you're becoming quite a racer. You just might end up racing at Talladega one day."

"I like the sound of that," said Shawn. "Then maybe I'd get to race against Johnny Pride."

Uncle Roy steered the golf cart into a large, open garage. He stopped the cart.

"Speaking of Johnny Pride," said Shawn. "When do I get to meet him? I can hardly wait."

"Well, there's something I need to tell you," said Roy. "The good news is, you get to be a junior race team member. The bad news is, I couldn't get you on Johnny's team."

"What?" exclaimed Shawn.

"I'm sorry, Shawn," said Roy.

Shawn looked away. He tried to hide his disappointment.

"That's okay, Uncle Roy. I know you tried your best," said Shawn. "So if I'm not with Johnny, then whose team am I on?"

"You're on Gene Pederson's team," said Roy, smiling.

"Gene Pederson? Mean Gene?" said Shawn. "You're kidding right? Uncle Roy, that guy stinks. He never wins. He's a loser."

"Who's a loser?" said a voice from over Shawn's shoulder. Shawn turned around. Standing directly behind him was a tall man dressed in a racing suit.

It was Mean Gene Pederson.

CHAPTER 3

HISTORY LESSONS

"Hey there," said Gene, sticking out his hand. "I'm Gene Pederson. You must be Shawn, my junior racer."

Shawn suddenly felt nervous. He didn't know what to say.

"Shake the man's hand," said Roy.

"Oh, sorry!" said Shawn, taking Gene's hand.

"Shawn, I'd like to show you around the track," said Gene. "Let's go for a walk."

"Okay," said Shawn.

"Have fun," said Roy. "I'll meet you back here around five o'clock. Think you can stay busy until then?"

"Oh, we'll keep him busy," said Gene. "Let's go, Shawn."

Gene headed out of the garage and into the bright sunlight. Shawn followed him.

"So, I hear you're a Johnny Pride fan," said Gene. He led Shawn past rows of semi trailers.

"You could say that," said Shawn. "Sorry about the 'loser' comment back there. I didn't really mean it."

"Forget about it," said Gene. "I can introduce you to Johnny if you'd like."

"Really?" asked Shawn. "Are you serious?"

"Sure," said Gene.

"Because, you know, he's like the best racer in the world," said Shawn, getting excited. "He's won the cup three years in a row. If he does it again this year, it will be a new record. That will make him even better than Richard Petty."

"You know your stuff, don't you," said Gene. "I've always been a bigger fan of Richard's dad, Lee Petty. He was a much better racer."

"No way!" said Shawn. "They don't call Richard 'The King' for nothing. And if you're going to go back to the early days of racing, you have to say Buck Baker was better than Lee Petty."

"Baker? Are you kidding?" said Gene. "Baker wasn't even as good as Tim Flock or Herb Thomas."

"Well, you're right about that," said Shawn. "Herb Thomas was the man. He would have won a lot more races if he hadn't gotten injured."

Shawn turned his head as six guys dressed in green race suits walked by.

"You sure know a lot about the old timers," said Gene.

"You do too," said Shawn.

"The way I see it," said Gene, "if you don't know the history of your sport, you can't make history. It's important to know how the sport has grown and changed so you know where it's going in the future."

"Good point," said Shawn.

"Come on, now," said Gene. "Follow me."

Shawn found himself standing right in the middle of Talladega Superspeedway. The track was fifty yards in front of him, just past a short wall. Beyond that stood the grandstand where all the fans would sit on race day.

Shawn was looking at a sight he had only seen on TV. And it was so much better in person.

CHAPTER 4

IN THE CAR

"This is awesome!" said Shawn.

"Pretty cool the first time you see it, isn't it?" said Gene. "But watch this."

Suddenly a group of eight men jumped over the wall in front of Shawn. They raced out toward the track.

Shawn looked to his right. A speeding stock car was coming toward them. It squealed its breaks and came to a sudden stop.

Shawn immediately realized where he was. He was standing next to pit road, the place where the pit crew made important improvements to the cars during a race.

The men in the pits quickly went to work. Two men used huge metal cans to put fuel in the car, one man raised the car up on a jack, and several men changed all four tires. And it all happened in a matter of seconds.

The car dropped back onto the ground and suddenly sped out of sight and back onto the track.

"That's 14.6 seconds," said a man standing in a tower above the pits. He was holding a stop watch. "That's not good enough, boys. We've got to get it under 13 seconds."

"Don't be so hard on the guys, Bob," shouted Gene. He turned to Shawn and said, "Bob's my crew chief. He keeps my team prepared and organized."

The man with the stop watch looked down from the tower. "I didn't see you there, Gene," he said. "But if I'm not hard on the crew, you won't win."

"Fair enough," said Gene.

"Let's do it again!" shouted Bob.

"Pretty cool, huh?" said Gene.

"Cool?" said Shawn. "That was the most awesome thing I've ever seen in my life."

"How would you feel about seeing it from the inside?" said Gene.

"What are you talking about?" asked Shawn.

"From inside the car," said Gene. "You can see how it feels to come in the pits from inside the car."

"Are you serious?" asked Shawn.

"I don't joke," said Gene. He made a serious face. "I'm Mean Gene, remember?" Shawn laughed.

Gene led Shawn over to Bob. "Can you get the modified ready?" Gene asked. "I want to take Shawn out."

"You got it," said Bob. He shouted to the crew. "Somebody bring out the modified right away!"

"What's the modified?" asked Shawn.

"It's a car that I built for my junior racers," said Gene.

"That's awesome," said Shawn.

"It doesn't go as fast as a regular stock car. It also has extra safety features so I can legally have a passenger in the car with me," Gene explained.

"He's the only driver who has one," said Bob. "You're lucky you were picked to be on Gene's team. None of the other junior racers are going to get out on the track."

"Not even Johnny's?" asked Shawn.

"Not even Johnny's," said Bob, laughing.

"Let's gear up!" said Gene.

Shawn sat in the back seat of Gene's modified stock car. He strapped on a helmet.

"Your helmet has headphones built into it," Bob told him. "You'll be able to hear Gene talking to you."

As Gene eased the car onto the track, Shawn heard Gene's voice in his headphones. "We'll take the first lap slow," Gene said. "And then I'll drop the hammer and see how fast this car can go."

Gene guided the car gently around the first two turns. But on the back straightaway, he started to accelerate. By turn number three, Shawn could feel his blood pumping as the car banked sharply around the turn.

"In a real race, there would be forty other cars out here and we'd be going twice as fast," Gene said.

Shawn could feel Gene push the car even faster. Shawn felt a rush. He tried to imagine 100,000 people in the stands cheering for him.

"Okay," said Gene. "We're pulling into the pit."

Gene ran another lap, sped the car around the last corner, then shot onto pit road. He slammed on his breaks, and the crew jumped at the car from out of nowhere.

This time Shawn looked down at his watch as the men did their jobs. Shawn counted to ten, eleven, twelve. Suddenly the car dropped off the jack, and Gene was punching the accelerator.

"I think they were faster that time!" shouted Shawn.

"I think you're right," said Gene.

A huge smile covered Shawn's face as Gene pushed the car hard around the track.

CHAPTER 5

A PIECE OF TRUTH

"I can't wait to meet Johnny," said Shawn as he and Roy rode the golf cart toward the track. It was Shawn's second day at Talladega Superspeedway. It was also media day. All the racers were at the speedway to answer questions from reporters. Gene had told Shawn that today he would introduce him to Johnny Pride.

"Johnny Pride," said Roy. "Do you ever think about anything else?"

"He's the best, Uncle Roy," said Shawn. "He's going to win four cups in a row. That's never been done before."

"Yeah, I know," said Roy. "The cups are important. But he's not the only racer out there. You got lucky getting placed with Gene. He's a great guy."

"It was cool how he took me on the track with him yesterday," said Shawn.

"No other drivers do that, you know," said Roy.

"I know," said Shawn. "But I still can't forgive him for putting Johnny in the hospital last season. He could have ended Johnny's career."

"I don't think you know the whole story," said Roy. "That accident was proven to be caused by a mechanical failure."

He continued, "Gene didn't crash into Johnny on purpose. Gene felt so bad about that crash, he hired a new crew chief."

"He did?" asked Shawn. "How come they never said that on TV?"

"Because the reporters on TV like to have a bad guy," said Roy. "They want Johnny Pride to have an enemy on the track. It's good for TV ratings. More people watch the races."

"It doesn't matter to me," said Shawn. "I would watch Johnny no matter who he's racing against."

Roy eased the cart to a stop. "Here we are," he said. "Are you ready to meet your hero?"

"I couldn't be more ready," said Shawn as he flashed a big smile.

CHAPTER 6

MEETING JOHNNY PRIDE

"Pretty crazy, isn't it?" Gene asked Shawn. The two were surrounded by dozens of racers in the middle of the media tent. "I'll go into the next room soon to take questions, but for now, we just have to wait," Gene explained.

"That's okay," said Shawn. He turned and looked through the crowd of racers in the room.

"Looking for Johnny?" asked Gene.

"Sorry," said Shawn.

"Don't worry about it," said Gene. "He's over there." Gene pointed toward a corner of the tent. "Come on."

Gene and Shawn walked through the crowd and across the floor of the media tent. "Hey Johnny," said Gene. "There's someone here I'd like you to meet. This is Shawn Lewis, my junior racer."

Shawn stepped forward. His heart was racing.

Johnny looked at Shawn. "Nice to meet you, bud," said Johnny.

"It's great to meet you, Johnny," said Shawn. He couldn't believe he was actually talking to Johnny Pride.

"So, you're a fan of Mean Gene, huh?" Johnny asked.

"Uh, yeah," said Shawn. He looked back at Gene.

"Actually, Johnny, you're his favorite racer," said Gene.

"Well, that's not a surprise, is it?" said Johnny, smiling.

He looked around at members of his racing team and added, "Everyone loves a winner, right?" His team laughed.

"I'd love to get your autograph," said Shawn.

"For sure," said Johnny. "Give me your cap."

"Great! I can't wait to add it to my collection," said Shawn. He handed Johnny his baseball cap. "I'm trying to get autographs of all the cup winners," he added.

One of Johnny's team members handed him a silver marker. Johnny signed his name in big letters on the brim of Shawn's cap.

Shawn was so excited, he couldn't stop talking. "Thanks to my uncle Roy, I've got eight other autographs already," he said. "I even have Tim Flock's autograph. My uncle bought that one for me online."

Johnny frowned. "Tim Flock?" he asked. "Is he a racer?"

Shawn laughed. "That's a good one," he said. "But Gene thinks Herb Thomas was the best of the old timers," he went on. "Can you believe that? Buck Baker was way better, don't you think?"

"Who?" asked Johnny, handing the cap back to Shawn. "Buck who?"

"Buck Baker," said Shawn.

Johnny frowned again.

Shawn added, "You know, the winner of the cup in 1956 and 1957."

"Never heard of him," said Johnny. "I don't really know about those old guys, Shawn. I live in the present. I let the bookworms worry about the past."

Shawn turned to look at Gene. Gene just shrugged his shoulders.

"Anyway," said Johnny, "did Gene take you out on the track?"

"He sure did," said Shawn, getting excited again.

"So I guess you got to ride in the granny car, huh?" asked Johnny.

"The what?" asked Shawn.

"The granny car," said Johnny. He grinned at his team again. "That car he drives around the track like an old grandma." His team laughed.

"Um, I guess," Shawn said.

"You want to see a real car go around the track?" said Johnny. "You come hang with me tomorrow. See you later. It's time to meet my fans."

Johnny strutted off toward a group of reporters.

CHAPTER 7

DISAPPOINTMENT

"Are you going to hang with Johnny tomorrow?" asked Gene as he and Shawn left the media tent.

Shawn didn't say anything. He kept his head down while he walked.

"Are you all right?" asked Gene.

"I'm fine," said Shawn.

"Don't let it get to you," said Gene.

"Don't let what get to me?" asked Shawn.

"The way Johnny acted back there," said Gene.

"It's no big deal," said Shawn.

They kept walking toward the garage. "It's not easy when we meet our heroes," said Gene. "They never measure up to our high expectations."

"They sure make Johnny seem different on TV," said Shawn. "I thought he was a nice guy."

"Johnny is a nice guy," said Gene.

"He didn't act nice," said Shawn. He kicked a rock across the pavement. "Why are you sticking up for him, Gene? Why are you defending him? He called your car a granny car. I wanted to punch him for saying that."

Gene shook his head.

"That wouldn't have done much good, kid," said Gene. "Johnny's just young, that's all."

"He didn't know anything about the old-time racers," said Shawn.

"He'll learn to respect the sport more as he gets older," said Gene. "That's what happens."

Shawn looked at Gene. "Can I ask you a question?" he asked.

"Sure," said Gene.

"Uncle Roy told me that your crash with Johnny last season was caused by a problem with your car and that you didn't do it on purpose," said Shawn. "Is that true?"

Gene nodded. "Yeah, it is," he said.

Shawn stopped walking. "Then why didn't you tell me that?" he asked. "And why didn't you go on TV and tell everyone else?"

"I don't like spending my time talking on TV," said Gene. "I just like to race."

"But everyone calls you Mean Gene," said Shawn. "Everyone hates you."

"Really? They hate me?" asked Gene.

"Well, I don't know," said Shawn. "Maybe they don't hate you, but they don't like you very much either."

"That's just the media hype and buzz. All I can do is be myself," said Gene. "True fans will figure out that I'm a nice guy. I won't be Mean Gene forever."

"I hope you're right," said Shawn. "But for now, can I give you some advice?"

"Shoot," said Gene.

"You should smile once in a while," said Shawn. "The fans like that."

"I'll give it some thought," said Gene.

Shawn laughed. Gene smiled, and they walked into the garage.

CHAPTER 8

RACE DAY

Race day was even better than Shawn imagined it would be. As Roy drove him to pit road, Shawn couldn't believe what he was seeing.

There were people everywhere. Crew members rushed wildly from their trailers to the track. People were grilling hamburgers and hot dogs next to their RVs in the middle of the speedway. And thousands of fans were in the grandstand bleachers waiting for the race to begin.

"Hey Shawn," said Bob as Shawn and Roy pulled into the pits. "Glad you could make it."

"Thanks for letting me hang out on pit road," said Shawn.

"Gene wouldn't have it any other way," said Bob. "Now, hustle back to the dressing room and get ready."

"Get ready for what?" asked Shawn.

"You're a team member," said Bob. "You need to put this on and get ready to go to work." Bob held up a full driver's suit. It was just like the one Gene wore.

"Awesome!" said Shawn.

"Hurry up and get ready," said Bob. "You're our junior race member. We need you."

As soon as he was dressed, Shawn settled onto a stool behind the pit wall to watch the race. Bob gave Shawn a set of headphones so he could listen to the conversations between Gene and his crew during the race.

Gene was having a great race day. Just twenty minutes into the race, he was only a few cars behind Johnny.

On lap 55, Gene's car came into the pits and recorded the fastest pit time of the day. Gene gave a thumbs-up to Shawn as his car flew back onto the track in second place. Johnny was still in first.

Finally, on lap 150 Gene made an amazing move to the outside and took Johnny by surprise. He pushed his car past Johnny's and snagged a lead that he never gave up.

Mean Gene finished the race several seconds ahead of Johnny Pride and won the Talladega Cup.

"Gene's the man!" shouted Shawn as Gene crossed the finish line. "Gene Pederson is the man!"

Gene took his car for a victory lap around the track, holding the checkered flag out his car window. Then Shawn watched as Gene crawled out his window and got sprayed and splashed with energy drinks by his crew.

After several minutes of celebrating, Gene stepped onto the podium to accept the Talladega Trophy. The race sponsors presented Gene with a huge gold cup. Gene raised it above his head as cameras flashed all around.

CHAPTER 9

CELEBRATING VICTORY

When the cheers had died down, one of the race officials climbed onto the podium with a microphone to interview Gene.

"So, Gene," said the official. "How does it feel to win your first cup race?"

"It feels great," said Gene. "Even better than I thought it would. But I've got to say, I've been proud of all my races this year. This just happened to be the first one I got lucky enough to win."

"When you won today, you beat fan favorite Johnny Pride," said the official. "Are you worried that his fans are going to like you even less after this race?"

"Johnny's a great guy," said Gene. "He's a top racer, and he has millions of fans. He's a good friend, and I respect him. But today I just happened to get lucky and beat him. The next race he might beat me. He makes me better, and I think I make him better."

"No more Mean Gene Pederson?" asked the official.

"If you want to keep calling me Mean Gene that's up to you," said Gene. "But my fans know who I really am." Gene looked out into the crowd. "Isn't that right, Shawn?"

The official looked confused. "Who's Shawn?" he asked.

"He's my junior racer," said Gene. "And I hope he would say he's my newest fan."

Gene looked back at the crowd. "Shawn, are you out there?" he called out.

Shawn stood up as tall as he could. The people in the crowd looked around to see who Gene was talking to. Shawn raised his hand. "I'm right here!" he yelled.

"Get up here, Shawn!" Gene said.

A path opened up as Shawn worked his way to the front of the crowd. He climbed onto the podium and stood next to Gene.

Gene shook Shawn's hand as fans cheered. Then Gene said, "Shawn, this is for you."

Gene pointed at his mouth. Then he grinned the biggest grin of his racing career.

Shawn smiled back.

CHAPTER 10

TOUGH COMPETITION

Back at Shawn's hometown kart track, Shawn headed into the garage. As he walked in, he saw his biggest rival, Freddy.

"Hey, Freddy," Shawn called, jogging over to Freddy.

"What's up?" said Freddy, turning around.

"I want to talk to you about your driving," said Shawn.

"My driving?" asked Freddy. "I don't think I care what you have to say about my driving."

"Listen," said Shawn. "I'm sorry for being a jerk before."

Freddy looked surprised. "Why the change?" he asked.

"After spending time with Gene Pederson last week, I figured out that trash talking and bragging about winning isn't cool," said Shawn.

"Gene Pederson? Mean Gene?" asked Freddy.

"I don't call him that anymore," said Shawn.

"I thought you said Gene Pederson was a loser," said Freddy.

"I did," said Shawn. "But I was wrong."

"So what does this have to do with me?" asked Freddy.

"It has everything to do with you," said Shawn. "Like I said, I hope that you and I can be friends."

"That's cool, I guess," said Freddy.

"And friends share racing tips with each other, right?" asked Shawn.

"I suppose," said Freddy.

"Well," said Shawn. "I think if you try something different on your third turn . . ."

Shawn went on to tell Freddy about all the strategies he had used in past races to beat him. Freddy seemed grateful. He even thanked Shawn.

But now, Shawn knew he might lose.

Soon he was back on the track. He was racing against Freddy in the toughest race of his life.

With one lap to go, Shawn tried everything he could to get around Freddy. But Freddy wouldn't let up. At every turn, he stopped Shawn from passing him.

On the third turn, Freddy kept his kart under control. He banked it wide, and then shot quickly through turns three and four.

Shawn didn't have a chance. He watched as Freddy crossed the finish line in front of him.

After the race, Shawn took his place on the second-place podium as Freddy stepped onto the winner's spot.

Freddy accepted his trophy and smiled as several cameras snapped his picture.

"I bet you wish you hadn't given me that advice," Freddy said with a smile.

"Nope, I'm glad I did," said Shawn, laughing. "I'll get you next time. I'll just have to push myself harder to beat you. Like a good friend of mine once said, 'I make you better, and you make me better.'"

ABOUT THE AUTHOR

Growing up, Chris Kreie could stand in his back yard on Friday nights and listen to the sounds of the race cars at the speedway across town. Chris now lives in Minnesota with his wife and two children. He works as a school librarian and writes books in his free time. Chris likes to drive his car fast, but he always keeps it under the speed limit.

ABOUT THE ILLUSTRATOR

When Sean Tiffany was growing up, he lived on a small island off the coast of Maine. Every day, from sixth grade until he graduated from high school, he had to take a boat to get to school. When Sean isn't working on his art, he works on a multimedia project called "OilCan Drive," which combines music and art. He has a pet cactus named Jim.

GLOSSARY

accelerator (ak-SEL-uh-ray-tur)—a device that controls the speed of an engine

corporate sponsor (KOR-puh-reht SPON-ser)—a company that gives money to pay for cars and a team for a driver

disappointment (diss-uh-POINT-ment)—something that lets someone down

mechanical (muh-KAN-uh-kuhl)—to do with machines or tools

media (MEE-dee-uh)—forms of communication, such as television and radio, that reach large numbers of people

modified (MOD-uh-fied)—changed slightly

straightaway (STRAYT-uh-way)—the straight part of a race track

strategies (STRAT-uh-jeez)—plans for achieving a goal

MORE ABOUT

BUCK BAKER (1919–2002) was the first NASCAR driver to win back-to-back Grand National Championships in 1956 and 1957. After he retired in 1976, he opened a racing school, where another great — Jeff Gordon — drove his first stock car.

TIM FLOCK (1924–1998) won an impressive 21.2 percent of his NASCAR cup series champion races. In 1953, Flock raced with a monkey in the car. The monkey, named Jock Flocko, raced his eighth and final race when he escaped his seat and started clawing Flock.

LEE PETTY (1914–2000) won the first stock car race he competed in back in 1948. During his 10-year career he never placed lower than fourth place. He was the first of four generations of Pettys to race. Together, they are known as the "First Family of NASCAR."

NASCAR LEGENDS

RICHARD PETTY (1937–) is known as "The King" for his amazing career as a NASCAR driver. The son of Lee Petty, Richard won 200 NASCAR races in his 35-year career, which is a NASCAR record. He also holds the record for most wins in a row with 10.

HERB THOMAS (1923–2000) was a founding driver of NASCAR when it was started in 1947. He won the Grand National Championship in 1952 and 1953. Injuries from a crash in 1956 forced him to retire. Memories of Thomas live on in the 2006 movie *Cars.* He was the inspiration for the character Doc Hudson.

DISCUSSION QUESTIONS

1. How do you think Shawn felt when he realized that Gene heard him say that Gene was a loser?

2. Why was Shawn disappointed when he met Johnny Pride?

3. Freddy was Shawn's biggest competition. Why did Shawn give Freddy racing tips?

WRITING PROMPTS

1. Johnny Pride was Shawn's favorite driver. Write a paragraph about your favorite athlete.

2. Shawn knew a lot about racing legends. Research a former athlete and write a report on what he or she did to contribute to their sport.

3. Write a magazine article from Shawn's point of view about his week as a junior team member.

READ IN OVERDRIVE